The Day Scooter Died

Written by Kathleen Long Bostrom

Illustrated by Cheri Bladholm

Zonderkidz

Zonderkidz®

The children's group of Zondervan

www.zonderkidz.com

The Day Scooter Died
Copyright © 2005 by The Zondervan Corporation
Illustrations copyright © 2005 by Cheri Bladholm

Requests for information should be addressed to:
Zonderkidz, Grand Rapids, Michigan 49530

Library of Congress Cataloging-in-Publication Data

Bostrom, Kathleen Long.
   The day Scooter died : a book about the death of a pet / by Kathleen Long Bostrom.– 1st ed.
   p. cm.
   Summary: Mikey feels responsible for his dog Scooter's accidental death, but his parents remind him that the dog loved him best of all and they can still love each other, although Scooter is now with God.
   ISBN 0-310-70902-4 (hardcover)
   [1. Grief—Fiction. 2. Death—Fiction. 3. Dogs—Fiction. 4. Pets—Fiction. 5. Christian life—Fiction.]
I. Title.
   PZ7.B6512Day 2005
   [E]-dc22
                         2003027955

Zonderkidz is a trademark of Zondervan.

Editor: Amy DeVries
Art Direction & Design: Laura Maitner-Mason

Printed in China

05 06 07 08/MPC/4 3 2 1

In loving memory of my Uncle Larry,
who bought me my very first pet.
Kathleen Long Bostrom

To Larry, Sandy, and Isaac Bird for the partnership
together with June Schneiweiss and Smoochy.
Cheri Bladholm

To Nancy DeVos Stehouwer who has brought life
into my life and has taught me so much about
God's presence and unfailing love.
Thanks, Scott Stehouwer

BEFORE MIKEY WAS BORN, Scooter belonged to Mikey's mom and dad. They took him with them everywhere.

But after Mikey was born, Scooter became Mikey's dog. And Scooter went everywhere that Mikey went.

When Mom and Dad brought Mikey home for the first time, Scooter sniffed his toes, licked him on the nose, then curled up next to his crib. From then on, anyone who came to see Mikey had to get past Scooter first.

EVERY TIME MOM OR DAD took Mikey around the neighborhood in his stroller, Scooter trotted along.

Mikey learned to crawl trying to grab Scooter's tail.

He took his first steps holding onto Scooter's ears.

When Mikey learned to ride a bike, Scooter ran along beside him.

Scooter wasn't allowed to beg for food at the dinner table. But somehow, when it came time for dessert, Mikey made sure Scooter never got left out.

AFTER MIKEY OUTGREW his favorite green blanket, he gave it to Scooter. Scooter dragged the ragged blanket around the house until it was even more tattered and just perfect to curl up on for a nap.

At night before going to bed, Mikey knelt and said his prayers. Scooter sniffed his toes, licked him on the nose, and curled up right next to him—on the blanket, of course.

Before Mikey left for school in the morning, he played ball with Scooter. "Catch the ball, Scooter!" Mikey said, tossing an old yellow tennis ball up in the air. Scooter knew just when to jump to catch the ball before it hit the ground.

ONE SUNNY SATURDAY, Mikey and Scooter were playing catch in the front yard. "Catch the ball, Scooter!" Mikey laughed, tossing the old tennis ball up in the air. Time after time, Scooter caught the ball before it hit the ground.

Then—Scooter missed.

The ball bounced on the sidewalk and into the street. Scooter jumped after the ball and caught it before it hit the ground a second time.

Neither Scooter nor Mikey saw the car until it was too late.

SCOOTER LAY VERY STILL. The ball dropped from his mouth and rolled away.

"Scooter! Oh, Scooter, please be okay!" Mikey cried. He knelt next to Scooter, who tried to lick his nose. But he couldn't lift his head.

Mom and Dad hurried out to where Mikey sat, his arms around Scooter's neck. "We'll take him to the animal hospital," Dad said. Mom ran into the house to get Scooter's green blanket to wrap around the injured dog, but by the time she got back, Scooter had stopped breathing.

"Wake up, Scooter! Wake up!" Mikey cried. Scooter did not open his eyes.

MOM AND DAD wrapped Scooter in the blanket. Dad took Scooter to the animal hospital and came home with only the blanket.

Dad washed it and dried it and folded it, then set it on Mikey's bed.

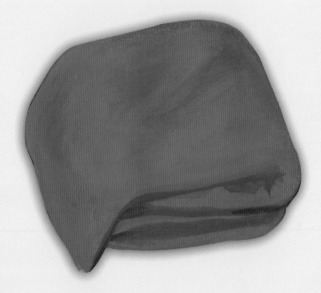

That night, Mikey could not sleep. He tried not to think about Scooter, but Scooter was all that he could think about. Scooter wasn't there to sniff his toes and lick his nose and curl up right next to his bed, on the green blanket.

Finally, Mikey wrapped himself in the blanket, curled up on the floor next to his bed, and fell asleep.

One night as Mikey was getting ready for bed, Mom and Dad came into his room.

"It's not the same around here without Scooter," Mom said.

Mikey just sat on his bed. He didn't say a word.

"We were thinking," Dad said, "about getting another dog."

"No!" Mikey cried. "I don't want another dog. Besides," he whispered, "it's all my fault that Scooter is dead."

Mikey began sobbing. "I threw the ball too close to the street. If I had been more careful, Scooter would be alive."

"It's not your fault," Mom said. "You didn't throw the ball into the street on purpose. It was an accident. And Scooter chased the ball because he loved to play catch."

"He loved to do anything with you," Dad said. "He loved you more than anybody else in the whole world."

"Really?" Mikey said, wiping his eyes.

"Yes, really," Mom said. "From the first day Scooter saw you, you were his best buddy."

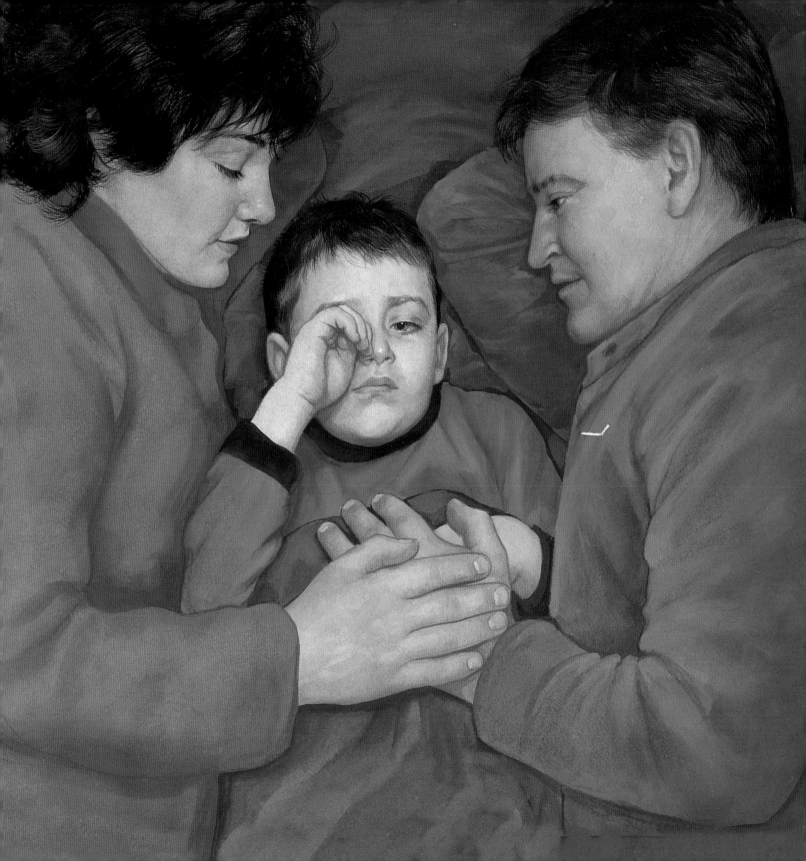

MIKEY STARTED TO CRY AGAIN. "Do you think Scooter is in heaven?"

Dad put an arm around Mikey. "Remember the story about creation? Well, on the same day God created people, God created animals—including dogs. All kinds of dogs."

Mom chimed in. "The Bible also tells us that at the end of time, all of creation will be made new. All creation includes every living thing."

"Including dogs?" Mikey asked.

"We'll just have to trust God to know what is best," Mom said. "But not even death can stop us from loving Scooter. Just like nothing can stop God from loving us."

THE NEXT DAY, Mikey got an empty cardboard box and took it to his room. He placed the old green blanket in the bottom. On top of that he put Scooter's collar and name tag and Scooter's favorite rubber bone. Last, he tucked an old yellow tennis ball in one corner. Mikey wrote "Scooter's Things" on the box with an orange crayon.

Kneeling next to his bed, Mikey prayed, "Thank you, God, for making animals. Especially Scooter. Please take good care of my best buddy. Amen."

Mikey was quiet for a little while, then he added, "P.S. God, you probably know that Scooter loves dessert. And catching tennis balls. And me. Scooter always loved me."

WHEN YOUR CHILD'S PET DIES

In this story we get a glimpse of a child who encounters the reality of death. Mikey's parents help him through the loss of his best friend, his dog, Scooter. They feel the loss too. Mikey's parents have no perfect answer about death; no one does. What they do have is a love for Mikey and a willingness to understand his sadness. They talk openly about Scooter. They recall memories of Scooter and Mikey. In this way they let Mikey know that it's good to remember Scooter and to think about him, even if it makes them feel sad.

Mikey's parents give him a valuable gift. They accept his feelings and let him know that even through the most difficult times, *God is there.*

As you read this book with your child, remember that this story might bring back memories for you. Feel free to talk about your memories, how you hurt, and how you handled this hurt. Talk about how Mikey felt when he played with Scooter. Talk about how scared Mikey felt when Scooter got hit by the car, how he felt it was his fault, and how important it was that he told his parents. If he hadn't told them, his mom and dad could not have helped him know the truth, that it wasn't his fault.

When we think about death, we need to remember life. Mikey's parents did this in three important ways. They talked about life with Scooter. They talked about life in the future without Scooter. They also talked about the life to come. While the explanation of whether Scooter is in heaven might be something for a theological debate, Mikey doesn't need a debate; he needs the reassurance of God's love for him and for his best friend.

Mikey comes up with a solution of his own for dealing with his loss. He puts things that remind him of Scooter in a very special place. For a child who is dealing with a loss, including the loss of a person, doing something like Mikey did is a wonderful way to work on going forward in life. And the one thing that Mikey's parents helped him to remember is God's love for him and his whole family and God's presence at all times—even when a loved one dies.

A WORD TO PARENTS AND OTHER CAREGIVERS

Everyday life in God's world presents challenges and problems for all of us. Children, as well as adults, struggle with a variety of feelings when faced with emotionally charged situations. By helping our children clearly recognize God's loving presence in their lives—that he is with them no matter what happens—we help to prepare them for life. One of the names of Jesus Christ is "Emanuel, God with us," and God with us is the pervasive theme of this Helping Kids Heal series. The books honestly and sensitively address the difficult emotions children face.

Children love a good story, and stories can provide a safe way to approach issues, concerns, and problems. Therapists who work with children have long used stories to help children acknowledge emotions they would rather avoid. When a loving parent, a kind grandparent, or a caring teacher reads about a story character who is experiencing difficult feelings, the child has permission to feel, to ask questions, to voice his or her fears, and to struggle with emotions. Remember, as with any good story, one reading is never enough. Repetition is a great reminder of the truths contained in the story.

Each child is different. Some children, when facing a difficult emotion, will ask questions and wonder aloud about the characters in the books. Other children are content to just listen and take it all in. After several readings, try to draw them out to talk about the story. You, more than anyone else, will know what the child needs. Keep these things in mind as you use these books:

• God is with you, too. You may be reading about something that is close to your heart. Your emotions may be as tender as the child's as you read the story. Pray that you will have a sense of God's loving presence in your heart.

- You do not have to know the perfect answer for every question, nor do you have to answer all of the child's questions. Some of the best questions are the hardest to answer. Be sure, however, to acknowledge the child's question. Be honest. Say that you don't have the answer. If the child asks, "Why did my pet die?" it's all right to say, "I don't know."

- Pray with the child to feel God's loving presence. Let the child know that you care about him or her and about his or her feelings. Let the child know that whether he or she feels God's presence or not, God is still with him or her. This is a loving, precious, and powerful gift that you can give the child.

- Be aware that God works in a variety of ways. You may not get much of a response from the child as you read this book. Don't be concerned. Read the book at different times. You are planting a seed—a seed for the child to recognize God is at work in everyone's life.

- Have fun! Enjoy the story and this time with the child. Children are precious gifts from God created in his image. God is helping you to prepare the child for a future in his kingdom.

Dr. Scott

R. Scott Stehouwer, Ph.D., professor of psychology, Calvin College, and clinical psychologist